ISBN: 9798989636976

Published by Big Bricks Publications

Edited by Shawna Brim for Ladies of Lit

Cover design by Israr Khan

PROLOGUE

I didn't know what to expect from this impromptu talk with Evette. She barged into the living room to force a conversation upon me at the exact moment that I reclined in my sofa chair and opened to the first chapter of Sins Of My Brother by one of my favorite authors, Aleya Mishell. I'd bought the book from Amazon a couple of weeks back and intentionally waited to read it until I had a day off where I had nothing to do. That way, I could spend an uninterrupted afternoon enjoying it from beginning to end. Evette noticed the annoyed look on my face that clearly conveyed I was not in the mood to deal with anything that might kill the chill vibe I was going for. She pressed on anyway, as if whatever she had to say couldn't wait.

"I've wanted to share something with you for a while, and I think now's a good time for you to hear it," said Evette.

"I was really trying to have an incident-free day," I grumbled.

"Please, Miles. It's important."

"Alright, I'm listening," I surrendered, exhaling an irritated sigh and setting the book down a little bit harder than necessary.

I brought the recliner back to its upright position as Evette settled onto the couch beside me. She paused for a moment, seeming to collect her thoughts, before speaking. My displeasure of being dragged into this conversation started to fade, replaced by concern, as it was clear that whatever she had to say was serious, and it was weighing on her. Giving her my full attention, she revealed some shocking news about what happened to her on the night she was away on a business trip a few years back that eventually ended our relationship.

"He put something in my drink. I don't remember exactly what took place, but when I woke up the next morning and he was lying in bed next to me, I didn't know what else to think but that we had consensual sex."

"How did you find out?" I inquired.

"He bragged about it to some guys at the office, and one of them reported it to H.R. With him being a high-level executive, rather than fire his ass, they brushed it off as a misunderstanding and wanted to transfer me to the Atlanta office. When I refused, I was offered a severance package but would've been required to sign a non-disclosure agreement to keep it quiet. I turned it down and instead decided to quit."

"Why is this the first time I'm hearing of this?"

"I wanted to tell you, but you wouldn't talk to me."

"That's because I thought you cheated on me. I had no idea you were raped."

"I tried several times, but then there was Sherie and after that, Tralisha," she emphasized sarcastically.

"Why would they have anything to do with you sharing something that significant to me? I would have never ended our relationship if I knew this," I confessed.

I could feel my blood pressure rising. I was a bit upset that she'd kept this from me, but I quickly calmed down when considering that she'd had to live with the agony of this terrible experience. Her expression was blank, and almost hollow, letting me know that this wasn't easy for her to talk about. I stood from my recliner and reached for her hand, gently pulling her up, so we could embrace.

"I'm sorry this happened to you," I whispered.

"Thank you for saying that. It really means a lot to me that you're not angry about this," Evette sobbed, melting in my arms.

"Well, I'm a little upset," I said with a smirk. "You've spoiled my day to relax. How am I supposed to concentrate on my book now?"

"If you can spare a few more minutes, I bet I can put your mind in a better space.

"Woman, please. Your cookie might be delicious, but you know damn well that's nowhere near enough time to satisfy the Hulk."

"No, fool. I wasn't referring to that. There's something else important I want to share."

"Come on now, Evette. I wasn't in the mood for any of this today," I complained.

"I know, but I promise you won't mind hearing what I have to say," Evette responded with excitement.

We settled back into our seats. Then, she continued with what took place after she quit her job. She reminded me of the day years back when she came by to retrieve the box she'd left in the bedroom closet. Turns out, aside from the heavy box causing me excruciating pain, inside it were important documents she needed to retrieve for an attorney that was helping sue her former employer for workplace harassment. After three years of litigation, the case was settled, and Evette was awarded a seven-figure payout.

"Now that you're a rich woman, what are your plans?" I inquired.

"Honestly? I was thinking of buying a house."

"The market's steady right now. Smart move."

"Would you look at some with me?" she asked.

"Of course. You know I'd help out in any way I can."

"Actually..." She paused, swallowing hard. "Would you join me in looking at a house for us?"

I fell silent, caught off guard. Staring at her, I searched her face for seriousness. Evette looked like she was holding her breath, anticipating my reaction.

"Yes, let's do it," I said finally after leaving her hanging for what felt like thirty seconds or more.

"Really? You mean it?" Her eyes lit up.

"I really mean it," I replied, smiling.

I went on to share with Evette that spending so much time in the same space over the past year had softened me to the idea of being a couple again. The woman's touch she'd added to my bachelor pad—fresh flowers on the table, throw pillows I never would've picked, the scent of vanilla in the air—made it feel less like a dude's crib. It wasn't only my place anymore; it was our home now. Keeping it 100, I expressed that wherever she planned to be next, I wanted to be right there with her. Not just as her friend and roommate but also as her man.

"I don't know what to say," said an overjoyed Evette.

"I've heard that yes is the perfect response in moments like this," I replied with a smirk.

"Yes, smartass!"

"Well, since we're in the sharing mood, and before you go rushing to update your relationship status on Facebook, it's probably best I tell you what I've been up to these past months."

My demeanor shifted to somber, causing hers to as well, as I braced myself to explain the mess I'd been tangled in lately. Evette let out a long sigh and shook her head as if she already knew from my lead-in that most likely it involved yet another mishap with a woman I worked with. It was an uncomfortable conversation to have with her, especially right after sharing that I wanted to get back together. I was single when it all went down, so technically, it wasn't any of her business. Still, I figured it was better she heard it straight from my mouth rather than some half-true version making its way to her through someone else, like from my gossiping best friend, Cleon.

CHAPTER 1

The evening had been quiet, which was just the way I liked it. I was in a particular mood where the less I had to deal with, the better. Tonight, I had zero interest or energy when it came to this twelve-hour shift, especially with it only being just a few hours into my 7 p.m. start time. All I cared about right now was for my work duties to go according to plan and for clock-out time to hurry its ass up.

It was now 11:57 p.m., and soon there'd be one less thing on the checklist. The hotel restaurant would close at midnight, and after tidying up, I'd spend the rest of the early morning only needing to manage the front desk. Same as every other Friday night, I spotted Deneen at the bar again, though tonight, she wasn't alone. Seated closely next to her was another good-looking woman. They were lost in conversation, each one occasionally taking a sip from her wine glass when it wasn't her turn to talk. As I made my way through the restaurant, wiping tables and collecting dirty dishes, Deneen glanced my way and smiled brightly.

"Renay, this is Miles, the gentleman I was telling you about," said Deneen, her four or five glasses of Rosé making it obvious she was tipsy.

"Yes, you were right," Renay replied, a mischievous glint in her eye.

"Right about what?" I inquired.

"Just girl talk," said Deneen, both women giggling devilishly.

"I'd love to know what you pretty ladies are discussing about me, but unfortunately, duty calls. It was nice to meet you, Renay."

"Indeed, it is," Renay responded, winking then tipping her glass in my direction.

I nodded and walked off to resume cleaning. From across the room, I could still hear their whispers and laughter. It might have been about me, but it was hard to tell for sure, and I decided not to wonder about it anymore. My focus at the moment was to complete what I was doing as quickly as possible so that I could kick back in the front desk chair and watch something on Netflix for the remaining hours of my shift.

Whatever *girl talk* Deneen and Renay had going on was nothing for me to be concerned with anyway. I'd already come to terms with the fact that the spark I thought I shared with Deneen was nothing more than a misunderstanding. Seeing her here at the hotel every day for the past six months, we'd gotten to know each other quite well. When I learned she was bisexual and, in a relationship, I soured on the idea of her and I getting further acquainted. It had little to do with her having a girlfriend and more about her being involved with someone else. With the deceitful bullshit I'd been dragged through this past year, I couldn't allow another woman to lead me down a rabbit hole that in the end never worked out in my favor.

"*Ohhhh, Miles*!" Renay sang from across the restaurant.

I huffed to myself then glanced at my smartwatch for the time before heading over to see what she needed. When I arrived at the table, Renay asked for my help escorting Deneen, who had exceeded her drinking limit, to her room. I agreed to her request but radioed for a security officer to cover the front desk while I was away.

CHAPTER 2

When we arrived at the top floor suite, Renay tussled through Deneen's purse, searching for the keycard to unlock the door. She held it open for me so that I could assist her intoxicated friend inside. I'd never been this close in her personal space and, aside from the slight whiff of the wine she'd been drinking all night, Deneen possessed an earthy, fresh roses scent that instantly aroused me. My dirty mind wondered if her pussy matched the pleasing smell of her hair and skin, and I would love to find out for myself if I was correct.

"You're sweet for helping," Renay said, as I walked Deneen across the dimly lit room and gently laid her on the bed.

"It's no problem at all. She'll always get the V.I.P. treatment whenever I'm on duty."

"You don't say... does that generosity extend to her guests?"

"Absolutely! Is there anything else I can do for you before I leave?"

Renay walked over to me, placing a hand on my shoulder. Her fingers slowly tiptoed down my arm, which she grabbed to pull me close to her, our torsos now having no space between them.

"You should stay a while," Renay said, her tone and sly smile clearly suggesting what she meant.

"Yeah, we're not ready to say goodnight just yet," said

Deneen, to my surprise now alert and patting the bed as an invitation to sit beside her.

I glanced at Deneen, then Renay. They both were eliciting that dangerous kind of allure that would make any man crack under pressure. I paused long enough to question whether I was properly reading the vibe they were both giving. I could feel my heart thumping, and a bead of sweat trickled down my temple. I stood there frozen, part bashful, part dumbstruck, caught between two gorgeous, uninhibited women who were either testing me or indeed seducing me. Most dudes would've already been butt-naked with porn star confidence and their hard dick in hand, but me? I was giving Steve Carrell 40-year-old virgin energy in a moment that clearly called for me to be Wesley Pipes.

I sat down like a man stepping into a fantasy he wasn't sure he earned. My hands lingered in my lap, uncertain whether they had permission to touch either of them. Noticing my reluctance, Renay leaned in, her breath grazing my neck, while Deneen's hand casually found my thigh. Neither asked my permission; quite frankly, they didn't need to.

Renay climbed onto my lap and quickly kissed me. The wetness of her lips and sweetness of her tongue caused my thoughts to relax and my body to stop pretending it had any control over the situation. She grinded on me, her arms wrapped around my shoulders to steady her position. Deneen's hands slowly paced up and down both of our backs. She seemed content with letting Renay lead the foreplay, but after a few minutes, she had built up her desire long enough to finally join in.

"Y'all planning to save me a taste?" Deneen said softly in a sultry tone.

"Sharing is caring," Renay sassily replied, exchanging a deep, wet kiss with Deneen, before switching positions to allow her to take over straddling me.

I barely had time to be amazed at the visual of two women kissing before Deneen's lips switched to meet mine. Our kiss was soft and laced with heat. It wasn't as aggressive as Renay's, and it stirred up something inside me that felt more passionate and emotionally connected, which wasn't surprising.

Deneen and I had grown close over time, sharing the kind of honest, vulnerable communication that close friends or lovers would naturally have. I never expected I'd be in the midst of a threesome, but I once thought Deneen and I were attracted to each other and could interact in this manner. Maybe she felt the same but needed to add Renay in the mix to mask the infidelity she'd be guilty of after being sexually involved with me.

With my arms wrapped around Deneen's waist, my hands contoured to her hips and ass instinctively. Her soft moans humming against my lips told me I'd found a hot spot. So, I continued to take advantage of that erogenous zone, massaging her soft body parts, causing her to release the sexiest sounds a man would ever want to hear. Her moans seemed to also have Renay excited, whose perky tits were pressed against my back, while her arms were wrapped around my chest and her fingers fiddled with my nipples.

"Damn, we're really doing this?" I muttered.

"Hell yeah!" Renay purred, running her long, manicured nails across my chest.

"I've wanted to for a very long time but only if you're game." Deneen leaned in and whispered in my ear.

"Oh, I'm game."

"Then let's stop talking and get this party started," Renay urged, guiding me back onto the bed.

CHAPTER 3

"Wait, are you telling me you had a threesome?" Evette interrupted.

I clenched my jaw, irritated that she'd broken her promise to let me finish. But clearly, her shock mattered more than my revelation.

"Of all people, given what we've been through, I thought you'd understand. I'm not asking for your approval. I would appreciate a little patience while I explain. If I'd given you that same courtesy three years ago, maybe we'd still be together and none of this would've happened."

The judgmental look on her face softened. Us living together, doing things couples do, had blurred the lines and made it sometimes easy to forget that I wasn't her man. When I said it aloud, it must've hit hard. Her shoulders slumped, and she turned away, trying to hide the tears gathering in her eyes. A part of me wanted to console her to soften the blow. But I chose not to. If we genuinely wanted a future, we had to stop carrying the past around like a suitcase full of broken glass. That meant having the hard conversations, burying the insecurities, and never letting them resurface.

"Evette," I said, softer now. "If we're going to move forward, then there can be no more secrets or half-truths."

She didn't answer, just nodded, signaling her agreement to

continue. I laid out everything that happened with Deneen and Renay. With each detail, Evette absorbed the words, letting them bruise her quietly without asking for mercy. Her face told a different story. It was a louder expression than any outrage she could've voiced.

It took me forty-five minutes to tell it all. I spared her the more intimate parts of how erotically charged the encounter had been. For one unforgettable hour with those two beautiful, sexy women, I became a man I'd only seen in movies, embodying a Mandingo-like intensity I never knew I had, while the three of us let the cards fall wherever they chose to land. Evette didn't need to hear all of that. Truthfully, she already knew too much. When I finally went quiet, she took it as her chance to speak.

"The way you talked about Deneen... it sounded like you had feelings for her."

"Yes, I did." I chose not to dodge her accusation, especially after insisting there be nothing hidden between us.

"Do you still?"

I didn't answer right away. My mind drifted back to when I first met Deneen. We connected fast, and there was an energy between us I couldn't quite explain. It felt as if we'd known each other in another life and were picking up right where we left off. The intelligent conversations, the laughter, the physical attraction, and the common ground we shared all felt like something dangerously close to love.

But after Deneen told me she was in a committed relationship with another woman, my interest in her shifted. I'd experienced infidelity from both sides—betrayed by Evette and entangled with Sherie while she betrayed her husband—so I'd grown wary of being anywhere near a situation like that. It was not guilt that haunted me. It was the chaos and the karma that followed. That kind of intimacy, whatever its intentions, carried a weight that left a bad taste in my mouth.

"There's nothing to worry about when it comes to Deneen. It's past tense as far as I'm concerned," I said bluntly.

"Where is she now?" Evette asked.

"Before I get to that, let me tell you what happened next."

CHAPTER 4

It was 4:45 p.m. on Sunday when the alarm on my iPhone blasted through its speaker exactly as I had programmed it. After grinding through back-to-back twelve-hour overnight shifts, I usually slept through most of the day. Thankfully, my manager, Joe, would allow me to crash in one of the hotel's vacant rooms. It spared me the danger of driving home forty-five minutes half-conscious; it also saved me from the near certainty of sinking into a hibernation so deep I might not wake in time for my next shift.

Now that I was out of bed, I decided to go for a walk before reporting for duty at 7 p.m. Behind the hotel was a trail nestled between desert brush and tall cottonwoods, leading to a man-made lake that glimmered in the late afternoon light. Being an avid nature and water lover at heart, I often walked the trail as a way to clear my mind, letting the quiet settle my thoughts as I escaped the constant noise of people and city life. As I started down the trail, I could hear Deneen call out to me from behind.

"Mind if I join you?" she asked, falling into step beside me.

"Don't mind at all," I said, smiling brightly.

We walked in rhythm, our heavy breathing and the gravel crunching underfoot filling the pauses in between the conversation. Neither of us mentioned what took place just twenty-four hours before. Instead, we chatted about her growing up in Tacoma, Washington and how her career with Banner Health landed her a remote assignment in Arizona.

"What's the deal with Renay?" I inquired, being nosey.

"She's my life partner. Being away for so long isn't easy, but we make it work."

"Is what happened last night the way you two make it work?"

"It's something we've wanted to do for a while."

"Oh, I see. That means any dick would've worked for the occasion." I stated, not asked.

"Maybe for Renay."

"Then what was it about for you?"

The path ended, as the lake came into view. Our focus shifted momentarily to the rippling water not too far from our shoes. We made our way to a nearby bench, sitting closely in silence for several minutes while continuing to absorb the perfectly beautiful sight of nature in front of us—our reward for the thirty-minute activity we'd just completed. Deneen gently rested her hand on my thigh. I hesitated but soon let my fingers trace across her skin, drifting toward hers until they touched and finally interlocked. I turned to face her, catching the softness in her eyes telling me everything she wanted to say without needing to speak.

"I'd rather not talk about this," she whispered.

"That's cool." I exhaled, slightly disappointed.

"I just want to be here...in this moment...with you."

Her eyes searched mine for acceptance. I nodded, choosing to digress silently rather than give voice to my discomfort with the situation. When it came down to it, just being here with Deneen was enough. If moments were all she could spare, I would welcome them because the alternative of not having her at all was the possibility I least wanted to have.

This was beginning to feel all too familiar; it echoed the past affair I'd had with Sherie. The players were different, but the game was the same. For a moment, my conscience shouted at me to quit while I was ahead. However, another look into her pretty brown eyes drowned out the voices in my head, and I chose instead to accept the complexity of attaching myself to Deneen.

"I'm right here with you," I concluded, leaning in to meet her lips for the type of deep, wet kiss that, while it lasted, made us both forget about Renay.

CHAPTER 5

Over the next few months, Deneen and I made our walks a regular ritual. Originally, it was meant as a way to reach our 10,000 steps per day goal, but it soon became something deeper. We would share life stories while holding hands and walking so close together that it felt as if we were joined at the hip. The spark of intimacy between us would usually become impossible to ignore. Lingering hugs and subtle kisses often escalated into me fingering her pussy and her stroking my dick. When we were certain no one was in sight, we'd peel down our sweatpants and sneak in a quickie before making our way back to the hotel.

"You sure do spend a lot of time with her," implied Nafula, surprising me from behind, as Deneen and I parted ways.

"Mind your damn business!" I quipped.

"She's the reason you don't have time for me. I'm not a fool."

"That's exactly what you are if you believe I have anything for you. I've told you numerous times. I ain't interested!"

"So, we make love and then you throw me away like I'm trash," Nafula whined.

"Look, what happened between us was a mistake. I'm sorry it didn't work out, but you need to get over it."

Her face hardened with a mix of anger and hurt, but her obsession beneath it was sharper still. She was now a woman scorned, and the look she gave me before walking away told me our ordeal was far from over. That look cut into me like a dagger to the chest, a reminder of how thin the line between love and hate could be. Once, in my eyes, Nafula had been a regal queen of Zamunda, elegant and composed, but now, she embodied the far more dangerous black panther, stalking and terrorizing its jungle prey.

My thoughts drifted to the first time I noticed her impeccable mocha skin, alluring hazel eyes, pearly white teeth, and full, prominent lips. It was easily her Kenyan accent that worked as the kryptonite that weakened me. Hook, line, and sinker—I took the bait. One thing led to another, and before I fully realized the entanglement I'd once again gotten myself into with a woman at work, we were undressing in the janitor's closet, and I was balls deep in her motherland.

Immediately after that, things between us went downhill. Before I could even zip my pants back up, Nafula was pouring out her heart, insisting she was in love with me. I saw that as crazy talk, given the light interaction we'd actually had, and instead of feeling flattered or sharing back the sentiment, I was turned off. The more she professed her devotion in the following weeks, the more I recoiled, realizing I wanted nothing to do with her. From then on, I did everything I could to make sure our paths didn't cross.

But her fixation didn't fade. It seemed to grow stronger. She began to do silly shit like leaving love notes at my workstation, brushing against me close enough for her perfume to cling to my shirt, and even more annoyingly, waiting at my car at the end of our shift, trying her damnedest to seduce me into another rendezvous.

There was nothing cute or sexy about it; in fact, it was more predatory than inviting. Every word, every touch, only pushed me further away. What she thought was irresistible felt suffocating, and I was desperate to escape her wrath before her relentless pursuit swallowed me whole, undermined my work performance, or caught the eye of management.

CHAPTER 6

Deneen had been away from the hotel for the past couple weeks on a business trip but was returning soon. She messaged me to say how much she couldn't wait to see me, and I replied that I felt the same.

DENEEN: *This meeting has me so stressed, and I could really use some of your kind of relief, if you know what I mean?*

ME: *I got you. Whatever you need me to do.*

DENEEN: *I love the sound of that! I'm not sure what time I'll arrive but be a good boy... let yourself into my room, be in bed, and have yourself ready for things to pop off as soon as I walk in the door. I'll handle the rest.*

ME: *Yes, ma'am, nasty girl!*

Grinning at the screen, I was so wrapped up in the sexting I had going on with Deneen that I was slow to notice a customer in the lobby who needed assistance. I dropped my iPhone on the desk and moved quickly to help. At the time, I thought nothing of it, but what I didn't realize was that leaving my device unlocked would open a door I never intended—one Nafula was all too ready to step through and take advantage of.

CHAPTER 7

I must have been in a coma-like deep sleep when Deneen arrived because I heard no signs of her entering the room or getting into bed. What did awaken me was the undeniable sensation of a woman's wet lips and tongue kissing, licking, and taking every inch of my dick into her mouth. Damn, Deneen must have really missed me. The oral pleasure she was giving me was by far the best I'd ever experienced with her. Scratch that, this was the best blowjob I'd ever received from anyone.

I tried several times to pull her up to me so that we could move past the foreplay, and I could show her my appreciation for the wonderful surprise she had given me. I wanted to make love to her until she was exhausted from the multiple orgasms I intended to give her. I knew exactly what sweet spot of her loins to reach and the right pace to drill her with in order to get her body shaking, and I was confident it would only take minutes to make it happen. But Deneen declined my offer each time I tugged at her, and with every attempt I made to stop her, she only sucked and slurped on my magic stick with more intensity.

She kept going, refusing to stop, even after I whispered through my panting that my body could take no more of what she was giving and that I would cum soon. Any moment now, I would explode, and if she didn't back away, I would have no choice but to release my masculine energy inside her mouth.

Deneen stayed where she was, continuing what she was doing, until every muscle of my body stiffened, and cum oozed from me. My shaft softened and retracted to half the size it had been just a minute before. My breathing slowed, my eyelids grew heavy, and I let out a big, uncontrollable yawn, as the itis suddenly kicked in. After that release and given what I was certain was an early hour in the morning, I was ready to get back to what I was doing before Deneen snuck in and slobbed me down. Before I drifted off, I made a quick mental note to thank her in the morning for the two-thumbs-up performance she had just delivered.

CHAPTER 8

The alarm clock jolted me out of my REM sleep. I felt rejuvenated, taking a moment to smile about the oral attention Deneen had recently given me. It was now 5 p.m., and I had overslept. I was surprised she hadn't woken me for our usual walk to the lake. She was nowhere to be found in the room, so I assumed she decided to let me sleep while she did some exercise alone. I didn't have time to figure out where she was because I needed to rush to my own room to quickly shower and get dressed for work.

When I made it to the front desk, I spotted Deneen in the dining lounge, working on her laptop. So, I walked over to greet her before clocking in for my shift. With a grin, I thanked her for the wonderful treat that had left me so relaxed that I overslept. She looked confused and asked me to explain, pretending that she had just arrived at the hotel and needed the stronger internet connection in the lobby to upload some documents before heading to her room. I assumed she was roleplaying—something we occasionally enjoyed doing to keep things flirtatious—so I played along.

"I must be mistaking you for someone else, or maybe my feelings for you are getting so involved that I dreamt you were giving me the best BJ I've ever had."

"Wow, the best ever? Then I am mad for missing out on

being a part of that action. But I could definitely make that a reality for you after your shift."

"Round two sounds good to me! I'm going to hold you to that," I replied with excitement.

She still looked at me, puzzled, as if she had no recollection that round one had even taken place. I scanned the dining room to make sure no one was paying attention to our interaction then swiftly leaned in to plant a big kiss on her lips. I was well aware of her relationship with Renay, but our bond felt real, and she treated me as such. I convinced myself that since Deneen was with a woman, technically I was her man, and I let that make sense enough for me to keep things going with her.

I couldn't discuss it with her right then, but soon, I would take the time to express my feelings and explain how difficult it would be to end things. It just seemed better, and easier, for us to figure out how we could make this crazy thing work. The way she treated me, despite being with Renay, made me believe she felt exactly the same and that she would be okay with going along with the arrangement.

CHAPTER 9

I had barely stepped into the back room when Nafula snuck up from behind and cornered me. Her sudden presence irritated me, and I wasted no time reminding her yet again that I had no interest in her. You would think that the harsh rejections would do the trick, but Nafula was relentless in her pursuit, never giving up, even after the umpteenth time of dismissing her.

"Nafula, I've told you several times. I don't want you," I spoke firmly, pushing her away, as I turned to leave. Before I could reach the door, her voice rang out, sharp with anger and attitude.

"You weren't singing that same tune this morning when your dick was in my mouth!"

I froze, stunned by the accusation. The words hit me hard and as the connection sank in I spun around, my face twisted in shock and disbelief.

"What the fuck did you just say?" I demanded.

Nafula crossed her arms, her smug look matched by a tone dripping with defiance, as she laid out the details of the encounter that I believed was with Deneen.

"I used my keycard to enter that bitch's room, the same bitch you lied to me about, and while you were asleep, I slipped into bed, kept my head under the covers, and I did what I knew she, or any other woman, couldn't do for you. I satisfied you in that way because I wanted to prove I could be any woman you desired. I love you that much, Miles."

My stomach dropped. The revelation hit me like a punch, and before I could even process it, Nafula stepped into my personal space, trying to hug and kiss me. That was the moment Deneen appeared around the corner. I assumed she caught only the part where Nafula confessed she loved me and most likely chose to only focus on just that, along with the touching and closeness she now witnessed. Her eyes narrowed, piercing me with her disappointment at the disturbing scene she walked into. I was given no time to explain that it wasn't what it looked like. A single tear slid down her left cheek before she turned and quickly walked away. I tried chasing after her, but as I reentered the lobby, customers were already waiting at the front desk, demanding my attention.

As I tried keeping my professional focus on my job, my mind was somewhere else entirely. Once again, I'd let myself get tangled up with a coworker, and as always, it was bringing me nothing but trouble. I damn sure should've known better than to have any dealings with Nafula, but I also should've kept to my initial thoughts about Deneen. I knew that getting involved with her was probably not the best idea, especially since she was already spoken for. Every time I thought I was building something special with someone, it ends up costing me more than it was worth. I despised Nafula for dismantling the romantic ties I had with Deneen and even more for the part she played in ruining the friendship we built.

I could already feel the weight of another mistake pressing down on me, and deep down, I knew that my time here at this job wouldn't last much longer. I would either leave on my own to escape the drama that was escalating or be fired because Joe forewarned me that one episode like this would be all it took to end my employment at the hotel. No matter how it played out, I'd already lost.

CHAPTER 10

I walked into Joe's office ready to give my resignation. My plan was simple—man up and put it all on the table before he found out on his own and fired me. At least if I quit, it would be on my terms. Before I could even open my mouth, Joe leaned back in his chair with a sigh.

"Heads up, we're short on the night shift. Nafula quit," he grumbled.

"She quit?" I blinked, caught off guard.

"Yeah. I didn't see that coming. Did she say anything to you about it?"

I swallowed hard, my mind racing. This was the moment I had planned to confess everything, but with Nafula already out of the picture, the timing felt different. Maybe even...lucky.

"Naw, that's news to me," I said carefully.

"So, what do you want to talk about?"

"It's nothing urgent. You've got more important things to worry about. We can talk another time." I forced a smile, brushing it off.

Inside, I was relieved. I didn't have to embarrass myself revealing the mess I'd created here at the hotel. Joe took a risk hiring me on as a favor to his frat brother, my former boss and our mutual friend, Marvin, and keeping hush about it all seemed like the only way I could save my job. Yeah, I was just going to let things be as they were without dragging myself down any further.

"Well, since you don't have anything pressing, I've got something I want to talk to you about." Joe leaned forward, resting his elbows on the desk.

"Oh, yeah? What's that?" I raised an eyebrow.

"Miles, I've been watching the way you handle yourself. The dedication you've shown, the way you step up to take on the big and little things around here. None of it goes unnoticed. You've been doing exceptional work, and I think it's time you take on more responsibility. I want to offer you the position of hospitality manager."

"Manager?" I repeated, believing I'd misheard him and sort of laughing at the shock of his words.

"You heard me right. You've earned it, and I believe you're ready," Joe clarified.

I sat back, trying to process what he was saying. After everything—the drama with Nafula, the heartbreak with Deneen, the mistakes I kept piling up—redemption was within my reach.

"Joe...I-I don't even know what to say," I admitted.

"How about yes, and thank you?"

"Hell yeah! Thank you, Joe. Really. I won't let you down."

"I know you won't." He nodded.

As I left his office, the weight I'd been carrying felt lighter, even if only for a moment. I couldn't help but reflect on how life kept playing out for me. No matter how many bad choices I made, no matter how many times I thought karma caught up to me and I'd reached my ninth life, somehow, I was still standing. Right then, I felt like maybe, just maybe, my Higher Power forgave me for Sherie, and second chances truly were given.

CHAPTER 11

Leaving Joe's office, I stepped into the lobby and instantly locked eyes with Deneen. She was sitting near the entry doors with her luggage at her side. I walked over quickly, needing to apologize to her about what recently went down.

"Deneen, what happened with Nafula..."

"You don't need to explain. We weren't committed to each other, and I am with Renay. It just caught me off guard, and it hurt because when I came back there to find you, it was to tell you that...I was in love. I wanted us to figure out how to have more going on than just those daily walks that turn into sex."

Her words hit me hard. Here it was, we both were similar in our feelings, but we didn't get a proper chance to share them with each other. I opened my mouth to respond, but she kept going.

"But after what happened, I had time to think. And I realized I don't want to end things with Renay. Nor do I want to keep being deceitful. So, I'm leaving. I need to go back to face her and tell her the truth about what we've been doing all these months."

"Deneen...I'll miss you. It's going to hurt not having you around," I said softly.

I stood there, stunned, wanting to convince her to stay, to fight for what we had, but deep down, I knew I shouldn't interfere any more than I already had. She gave me a sad smile. We embraced, neither of us wanting to let go, holding on to each other longer than we probably should have, given the professional setting we were in. But with the shuttle bus arriving outside, there was no choice but to part ways. As she walked toward it, she turned back one last time.

"Oh...I did something petty," she admitted. "I called an old colleague that works with the Department of Naturalization to find out about Nafula's citizenship status. Turns out her visa expired a few years back, and I was going to anonymously file a report, but instead, I confronted her and gave her the option to quit immediately and save her from further consequences. To be totally honest, I wanted to make sure she didn't have the opportunity to be near you ever again."

She stepped onto the bus and the doors closed behind her. I stood in the lobby watching the shuttle drive away. The silence that followed felt louder than anything she had said. Nafula was gone, which I was extremely grateful for, but now that Deneen was gone, all I had left was the hollow reminder that every choice I made over the last couple years when it came to women seemed to end the same—with me standing alone, wondering where I went from here.

CHAPTER 12

The room felt heavier after I finished sharing everything with Evette about what went down at the hotel. There were no bad reactions, no outburst of anger, no sign of tears, nothing that revealed she was disappointed nor supportive. She just sat there quietly, absorbing it all, her fingers laced together in her lap like she was holding herself still. But the silence between us wasn't awkward. It was the kind that came right before someone decided that they'd heard enough on that matter and just wanted to move on from it. Evette inhaled slowly then exhaled like she'd been holding that breath for days.

"Since we're having a full disclosure moment, there's something I need to tell you too."

"If you're about to tell me there's some dude you've been messing with..."

"Really, Miles? That's where your mind goes?" She cut her eyes at me so sharply that I needed to lean back in my recliner to brace myself for the impact of the verbal backlash I was sure to receive from her next.

"I mean, the dramatic pause is usually how bad news starts."

"True, but this isn't about another man. Just...let me talk."

That shut me up. Something in her tone made my chest tighten. She wasn't gearing up for drama. It sounded like there was something that scared her. Evette shifted on the couch, pulling her legs up beneath her like she needed to make herself smaller to get the words out. That gesture was my cue to perk up and give her my full attention.

"I really meant what I said earlier about wanting us to look at a house together. Before we go any further with that, you need to know what's been going on with me."

"Okay, so what happened?" I scanned her face for any clues of if whatever was going on was something good or something bad, but she stared at her hands to hide her emotions from me.

"A few months after I quit my job, I went in for a routine checkup. Nothing special, just something I'd been putting off. They found...something," Evette revealed.

"What do you mean by 'something'?"

"They found a lump."

"Evette..."

"I didn't want to worry you," she continued quickly, as if she needed to outrun my reaction. "And at the time, we weren't even talking. You were off living your life, and I was trying to figure out mine. So, I kept it to myself."

"What did the doctor say?" I hopped from my recliner to sit as close to her on the couch as possible. She finally looked up at me. Her eyes were glossy but steady.

"I was diagnosed with breast cancer."

The words hit me like a punch to the mouth. I was devastated and felt the air leave my lungs. I reached for her hand, but she pulled it back gently, like she wasn't ready to be touched yet. I understood her reaction because it matched the strong facade Evette typically liked to portray.

"I didn't want to tell you until I knew what I was dealing with. I didn't want your pity or you feeling obligated to come running back into my life because something was wrong with me."

"Come on now, I would never..."

"Let me finish," she whispered. I nodded, swallowing the knot in my throat.

"I went through the scans. Then the biopsy. Then more scans. Then the meetings with specialists. I kept thinking, maybe it's nothing. Maybe it's early and it's treatable. Things were going great. My doctor was optimistic. The cancer was in remission, and I've been feeling fine, but after some recent tests, my doctor revealed that it has again shown its ugly face."

"Why didn't you tell me sooner?" I asked as sensitively as I could.

"Because I didn't know if you'd want to deal with all of this. With the appointments, the treatments, the uncertainty. I didn't want to drag you into something that might break us before we even had a chance to fix what was already broken."

"You don't get to decide what I can or can't handle," I said, shaking my head, irritated and angry about finding out her diagnosis in such a way that I felt cornered and betrayed with the reveal.

"I know," she whispered. "But I was scared. I had already lost your heart, and I didn't want to lose you as a friend also."

"That could never happen! Doesn't matter what the hell we've been through, I will forever have your back when it comes to your wellbeing," I asserted sternly, firmly holding her hand. She blinked uncontrollably, a tear slipping down her cheek.

"You say that now..."

"I say that because it's true, and you don't ever need to think anything different."

"I start treatment next month." She let out a shaky breath.

"Okay," I said, nodding. "Then I'll be there with you."

"Miles..."

"I'll be there!" I repeated, more firmly. "Every appointment. Every follow-up. Whatever you need. I'm not going anywhere."

Evette covered her face with her free hand, her shoulders trembling. Not from fear but from relief. From finally letting someone else carry a piece of the weight. I pulled her into my arms, and this time, she didn't resist. She folded into me like she'd been waiting for this moment longer than she wanted to admit.

"I'm sorry," she whispered into my chest.

"Stop that shit right now. There is absolutely nothing for you to be sorry about."

"So, you're really sure about this? About us? Even with everything going on?"

"Evette, I just told you I wanted to build a life with you. You think cancer is going to scare me off? I'm not that dude. But I am the one who is going to annoy the hell out of you by asking a million questions about your treatment. I need to know that you, that we, are doing everything in our power for you to be the strong bitch that we both know you are and slay the fuck out of that evil dragon," I promised, brushing a tear from her cheek. She laughed—a soft, broken sound but a laugh, nonetheless.

"I should've known you'd turn this into a whole thing."

"Absolutely. I'm dramatic. It's part of my charm."

"Thank you for not freaking out." She squeezed her

forehead deep into my chest.

"Oh, I'm freaking out," I admitted. "Just internally, like a grown man is supposed to."

She laughed again, and this time, it sounded real. We sat there for a long time, holding onto each other, letting the reality of everything settle between us, coming to terms that cancer was not something that would break us but rather something we'd face together. The future didn't feel uncertain; I t felt shared.

I stole a moment to think about the time wasted between us since our breakup. I was mad at myself for not taking her numerous calls, changing my phone number, and cutting off her access to my home. Those were all times she could've told me what was going on—about the rape and the cancer. If I had heard her out then, maybe we would've never split apart. Maybe there wouldn't have been any other women. Maybe Sherie would be alive today. Fuck me! If I only had given Evette the opportunity back then to explain.

EPILOGUE

The bell above the barbershop door jingled as I stepped inside, and for the first time in months, the familiar scent of aftershave and hot clippers didn't feel comforting. It felt like walking into a life I wasn't sure belonged to me anymore. The fellas were in mid-debate about MJ, Kobe, or Lebron being the best basketball player of all time, but the moment they saw me, the noise softened like someone turned down the volume. Darius was the first to acknowledge me. He pulled me into one of those masculine hugs that men pretend are quick but hold on longer than they mean to. When he stepped back, his eyes were softer than usual.

"Damn, Miles...I'm really sorry about your lady. Evette was a good woman," he said.

"Yeah, she was. Thanks, D." I nodded, swallowing the tightness in my throat.

"Hard to believe she's gone. She used to come in here and clown all of us like she was one of the fellas," Marvin said, shaking his head in disbelief.

"Especially Cleon. She stayed on his neck," teased Joe, getting his beard lined up by Darius.

"First of all, sis joked with me because she actually liked me. Don't be jealous because y'all were just extras she pretended to care about," Cleon clapped back.

A few chuckles broke the tension, and I was grateful for it. I'd been grieving heavily over the past year but visiting my barbershop family and being able to laugh in less than five minutes of stepping into Goodfellas was already showing to be just what I needed to ease my mind a little. I sat in my usual chair, even though I didn't need a cut. I just needed...this. The noise. The banter. The sense that life kept moving even when mine felt stuck. Cleon draped the cape over me anyway out of habit.

"How you holding on, for real?" Cleon asked.

"I don't know. Some days, I'm good. Other days, I'm mad as hell," I responded then exhaled, long and shaky.

"Mad?"

"Yeah. I'm pissed that she carried that shit alone for nearly three years. I get why she did, but I still wish she'd told me sooner. Maybe us fighting it together would've worked."

"But you can't be..."

"Ain't no right way to lose somebody you love. It's alright to feel what you feel," said Darius, cutting off Cleon and giving him a narrow-eyed look that suggested he stop talking while he was ahead. Cleon understood and took heed.

"I wanted to apologize to y'all for being M.I.A. I didn't feel like talking back then, but I appreciate y'all for reaching out," I said.

"Son, we don't need your apology. We're family. We always got your back," emphasized Marvin, with everyone chiming in in unison to reiterate the same.

"Appreciate that, everyone. I wish Evette had people in her life like I have with y'all. Her parents already passed, no siblings, and no relatives that she kept up with. It was just me to comfort her in the end."

"Is that why she left you all the money?" Cleon untactfully blurted out.

"Cleon, what the fuck!" yelled Darius.

"What? I mean, all of us up in here already knew," defended Cleon.

"Any guess on how it is we do?" Marvin sarcastically joked, everyone eyeballing the only possible source of my personal business being exposed to the barbershop.

"Yeah, yeah, yeah. It was me," admitted Cleon. "But in my defense, you ain't say nothing about it being a secret."

"She did leave it for me," I answered after the laughter died down.

"What you gone do with it?" Cleon inquired.

"If you ain't about the dumbest..." Darius agitatedly responded.

I looked around the shop—the cracked leather booster chairs, the faded posters of numbered haircut examples, the men who'd been my unofficial family therapists for years—and I realized that although there was nothing but love flowing throughout the atmosphere, I didn't belong here anymore. Not at Goodfellas, not in this city, and not in this version of my life.

"I'm leaving," I said plainly.

"Leaving to where?" Darius inquired while lining up Joe's mustache.

"Anchorage."

"Alaska? You don't even like the cold. What about the bears? It ain't never dark there. Are you serious, bro?" The whole shop reacted at once.

"I know about all of that. It's something I've been wrestling with for years. I've always wanted to work in nature as a park ranger, but the pay's not great, so I talked myself out of it. Now that money ain't an issue, I'm finally gonna go for it. My life lately has been so chaotic, and I just want something that feels peaceful for once. And if I'm being honest with myself...right about now, I need a fresh start."

"So, you just gone leave me with these fools?" Cleon joked, crossing his arms.

"Pretty much," I joked back.

"Selfish!"

"I get it. Sometimes you gotta go where your soul can breathe," said Joe.

"When are you leaving?" Darius asked, feathering the loose hairs from Joe's neck and shoulders.

"Two weeks."

"Two weeks?" The shop again reacted in unison.

"Then we party before you go. All of us. Drinks, food, whatever. A proper send-off," Marvin suggested.

"Yeah," Cleon added. "We ain't letting you disappear into the wilderness without embarrassing you one last time."

"I'd like that." I smiled, feeling something warm settle in my chest.

"There. Fresh for Alaska. That'll be thirty dollars," said Cleon, as he pulled the cape off with a flourish.

"Put it on my tab."

"About that. Since you are leaving, we need to settle your bill."

The shop erupted in laughter again. For a moment, I let myself imagine Evette sitting at home on the couch, smiling like she always did when I shared with her my misadventures with the brothers at Goodfellas. I missed her. I'd probably miss her for the rest of my life.

Cleon closed the shop an hour early, and we all headed to Casino Arizona. When I stepped outside into the late-afternoon sun, I felt something I hadn't felt in months. Forward motion. A new beginning waiting somewhere far away, where the air was cold and clean, and the world was quiet enough for me to hear myself think. Alaska wasn't an escape; it was a promise—to live the kind of life Evette would've wanted for me. For the first time since losing her, that felt possible.

MORE TO COME

DID YOU ENJOY READING THIS BOOK?

Please help others enjoy it too.

Review it.
Recommend it.
Buy it for a friend.
Lend it.

Send me a message so that I can personally thank you by visiting the website: AndreBriscoe.com

OTHER RELEASES FROM BIG BRICKS PUBLICATIONS:

Bound By His Love

by Aleya Mishell

Misplaced Affections (Book 1 and 2)

by Aleya Mishell

Sins of My Brother

by Aleya Mishell

Regret Has A Name (Book 1 and 2)

by Aleya Mishell

Casual Encounters With Women From Work (Book 1 and 2)

by Andre Briscoe

www.ingramcontent.com/pod-product-compliance
Lightning Source LLC
LaVergne TN
LVHW010945110826
845149LV00013B/2763

* 9 7 9 8 9 8 9 6 3 6 9 7 6 *